Welcome to ALADDIN QUIX!

If you are looking for fast, fun-to-read stories with colorful characters, lots of kid-friendly humor, easy-to-follow action, entertaining story lines, and lively illustrations, then **ALADDIN QUIX** is for you!

But wait, there's more!

If you're also looking for stories with tables of contents; word lists; about-the-book questions; 64, 80, or 96 pages; short chapters; short paragraphs; and large fonts, then **ALADDIN QUIX** is *definitely* for you!

ALADDIN QUIX: The next step between ready to reads and longer, more challenging chapter books, for readers five to eight years old.

Our Principal Breaks a Spell!

Read all the ALADDIN QUIX books!

By Stephanie Calmenson

Our Principal Is a Frog!
Our Principal Is a Wolf!
Our Principal's in His Underwear!
Our Principal Breaks a Spell!

Royal Sweets
By Helen Perelman

Book 1: *A Royal Rescue*
Book 2: *Sugar Secrets*
Book 3: *Stolen Jewels*

A Miss Mallard Mystery
By Robert Quackenbush

Dig to Disaster
Texas Trail to Calamity
Express Train to Trouble
Stairway to Doom
Bicycle to Treachery
Gondola to Danger
Surfboard to Peril
Taxi to Intrigue

Little Goddess Girls
By Joan Holub and Suzanne Williams

Book 1: *Athena & the Magic Land*

★ Our Principal ★
Breaks a Spell!

BY **Stephanie Calmenson**

ILLUSTRATED BY
Aaron Blecha

Q QUIX

ALADDIN QUIX

New York   London   Toronto   Sydney   New Delhi

ALADDIN QUIX

Simon & Schuster Children's Publishing Division

1230 Avenue of the Americas, New York, New York 10020

First Aladdin QUIX hardcover edition May 2019

Text copyright © 2019 by Stephanie Calmenson

Illustrations copyright © 2019 by Aaron Blecha

Also available in an Aladdin QUIX paperback edition.

All rights reserved, including the right of reproduction in whole or in part in any form.

ALADDIN and the related marks and colophon are trademarks of Simon & Schuster, Inc.

For information about special discounts for bulk purchases, please contact Simon & Schuster Special Sales at 1-866-506-1949 or business@simonandschuster.com.

The Simon & Schuster Speakers Bureau can bring authors to your live event. For more information or to book an event contact the Simon & Schuster Speakers Bureau at 1-866-248-3049 or visit our website at www.simonspeakers.com.

Designed by Karin Paprocki

The illustrations for this book were rendered digitally.

The text of this book was set in Archer Medium.

Manufactured in the United States of America 0419 FFG

2 4 6 8 10 9 7 5 3 1

Library of Congress Control Number 2018959534

ISBN 978-1-4814-6675-2 (hc)

ISBN 978-1-4814-6674-5 (pbk)

ISBN 978-1-4814-6676-9 (eBook)

To the dedicated teachers and principals,

who perform magic every day

—S. C.

Cast of Characters

Mr. Barnaby Bundy: Principal

Dr. Olivia Martin: Sorcerer

Roger Patel: Top student and class leader

Ms. Ellie Tilly: Kindergarten teacher

Mrs. Gwen Feeny: Third-grade teacher

Ms. Marilyn Moore: Assistant principal

Hector Gonzalez: Loves making his friends laugh

Nancy Wong: Hopes to be a zoologist

Alice Wright: Kindergartener who always tells the truth

Contents

Chapter 1: Principal's Helper   1

Chapter 2: Zippity, Zoom!   6

Chapter 3: Catch That Broom!   14

Chapter 4: Help in a Hurry   23

Chapter 5: Breaking the Spell   33

Word List   43

Questions   47

1

Principal's Helper

Mr. Bundy is the principal of PS 88. He plans great assembly programs. He had just started planning a new one when a letter in a glittery envelope arrived.

Mr. Bundy quickly tore open the envelope. The letter said:

Are you looking for a **NEW** and **EXCITING** program for your students? Look no further!

The answer is right in your hands.

Sincerely,
Olivia Martin, DS

*A visitor from the department of **sanitation**—the DS—is just what PS 88 needs*, thought Mr. Bundy. ***Dr. Olivia Martin** can help us keep our school neat and clean.*

Inside the envelope was a packet that said *Dr. Martin's Magic Powder.*

Great! We can always use a free sample of cleaning powder, thought Mr. Bundy.

He was quite **impressed** and was about to read more when **Roger** knocked on his door.

"Hi, Mr. Bundy! What's my job today?" Roger asked.

Every couple of weeks, a different student had the honor of being the principal's helper. Today was Roger's turn.

"Welcome, Roger," said Mr. Bundy. He glanced at his watch. "I'm due at **Ms. Tilly**'s kindergarten class in a couple of minutes for a poetry reading," he said. "Here's what I'd like you to do while I'm gone."

Mr. Bundy had a stack of

newsletters on his desk for the PS 88 parents.

"Count out the correct number of newsletters for each class," said Mr. Bundy. "When you're done, please drop them in the teachers' mailboxes."

"Sure thing, Mr. B!" said Roger.

This job was a no-brainer. After all, Roger was one of the smartest kids in the school.

2

Zippity, Zoom!

As soon as Mr. Bundy left, Roger got to work. But he wasn't in any great hurry to count the newsletters. His classroom cleanup job for the day was to sweep. Roger *hated* sweeping, but his teacher **Mrs. Feeny** said he had to do it anyway.

He was trying to think of a way out of his sweeping job when Mr. Bundy's phone rang.

Ring-ring! Ring-ring!

Answering the phone was not one of Roger's jobs for Mr. B.

Ring-ring! Ring-ring!

I wish that ringing would stop, thought Roger.

He was **glaring** at the phone when a glittery envelope on the desk caught his eye. Next to it

was a letter with a packet that said
Dr. Martin's Magic Powder. Roger
knew the "don't read, don't touch"
rule for Mr. Bundy's helpers. But
this was too hard to **resist**!

He tried to peek at the letter
without touching it. That didn't

work. Suddenly, his hand took on a life of its own. It floated to the letter and opened it with the flick of one finger. Roger couldn't read fast enough.

The letter offered a "new" and "exciting" program for students. It was signed by a **sorcerer** named *Olivia Martin, DS.*

On the back it said *Enjoy your free sample—good for one job of your choice. Your students will thank you!*

There was a list of magic

spells and a phone number: *989-IMA-SORCERER.*

Roger studied the list. His eyes popped open when he saw "Magic Broom Spell."

"Wow!" he said aloud. "This is exactly what I need! If it works, I'll never have to do my job sweeping our classroom again!"

According to the instructions, all he needed to do was sprinkle a broom with the magic powder and say the magic spell.

Roger remembered that Mr.

Bundy kept a broom in his closet. He went and got it.

He felt bad about breaking the principal's "don't read, don't touch" rule, but **curiosity** was making his fingers itchy.

Suddenly, he was ripping open the packet, sprinkling the powder and saying the magic spell:

"Zippity, zap!
Zippity, zoom!
Get to work,
you lazy broom!"

In the blink of an eye, the broom jumped to life and started sweeping every inch of Mr. Bundy's floor.

Roger couldn't believe it. A broom sweeping with no person and no motor?

Amazing! It really was magic.

3

Catch That Broom!

When the broom finished the office—**ZIP!**—it flew out into the hall. Roger pinched himself to make sure he wasn't dreaming.

Ouch! He wasn't.

"Come back!" he cried.

Roger had to catch that broom before anyone—especially Mr. B—saw it!

But the broom was fast. It was faster than Roger. It zipped up one hall and down another.

It swept the whole first-floor hallway, then headed up the stairs with Roger racing behind.

"Stop! Please!" he called.

He thought he heard the broom say "Nyah, nyah!"

Uh-oh! Roger had just about reached the stairway

when **Ms. Moore**, the assistant
principal, appeared.

"Where are you going in such
a rush?" she asked.

Roger had to think fast.

"Um, my science project
got a little out
of hand," he
said. "It's . . .

it's a battery-operated broom."

"You are PS 88's very own Einstein!" said Ms. Moore proudly. "But even Einstein would not be allowed to run in the halls."

"Yes, Ms. Moore," said Roger.

Roger felt terrible about telling Ms. Moore a lie. But he had no time to think about that now. He had to catch that broom!

Roger raced up the stairs. On the second floor, his luck changed. He saw his good friends **Hector** and **Nancy** coming his way.

"You've got to help me!" cried Roger as the broom went **careening** around a corner.

"What was that?" asked Hector.

"There's no time to explain," said Roger. "That broom's under a magic spell, and we've got to stop it!"

"It's heading for the stairs!"
said Nancy. **"Let's go!"**

Roger, Nancy and Hector
followed the broom downstairs
and cornered it in the lunchroom. Thank goodness no one
was around to see what was
going on.

"Gotcha!" said Roger.

He grabbed one end of the broom. Nancy grabbed the other end. Hector held on in the middle.

They were trying to keep the broom still when—**SNAP!**—it broke in half. The kids fell back. When they looked up, they saw *two* brooms racing toward the stairs.

"Oh no!" said Roger. "This is going from bad to worse."

"Don't worry," said Nancy. "We'll catch them."

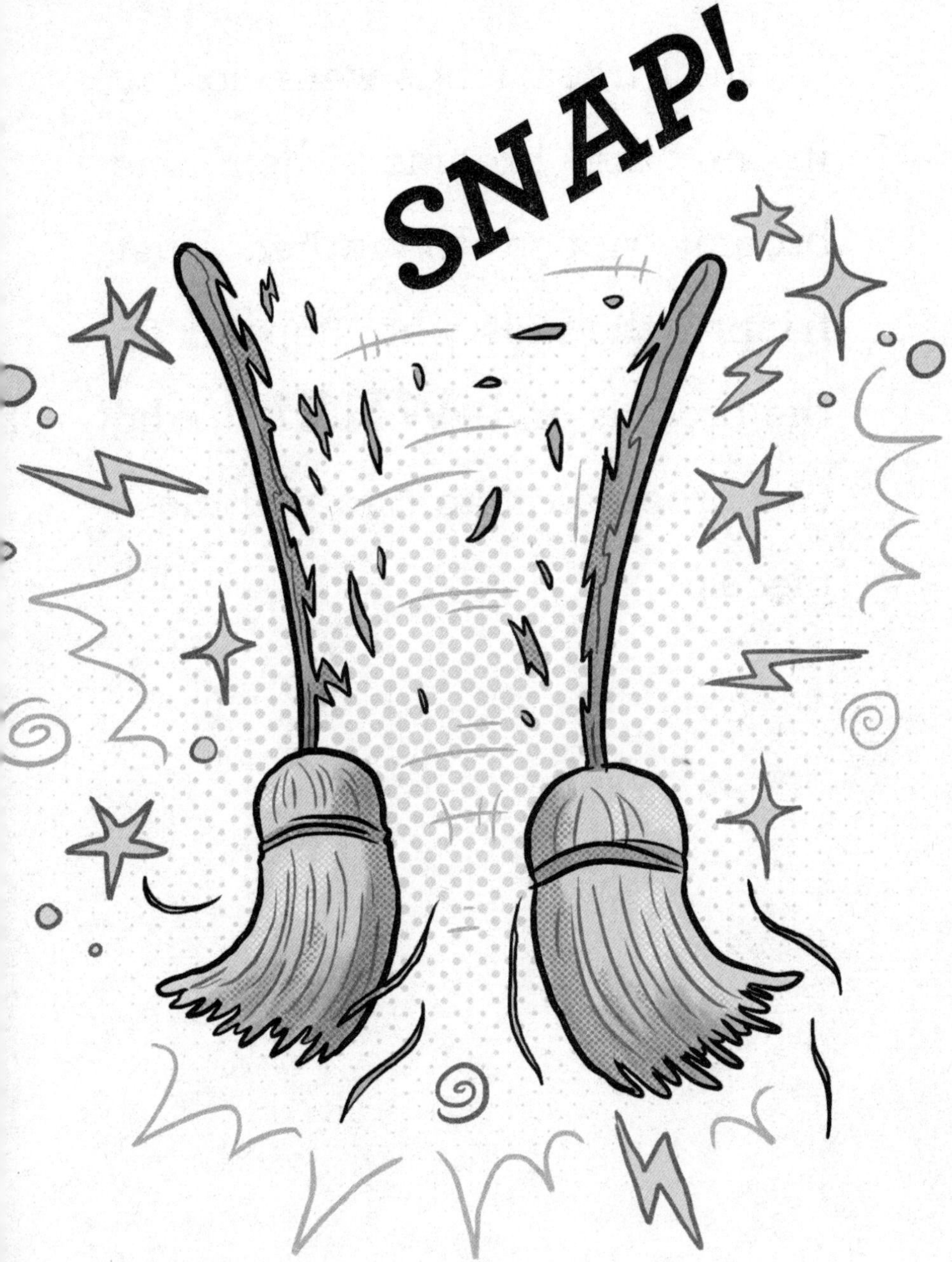
SNAP!

The three friends were closing in on the brooms when one broom tripped the other. That tripped the kids who stepped on the brooms and—**WHAM!**—the two brooms broke into countless pieces.

4

Help in a Hurry

The kids fell over one another in a heap and landed on top of the brooms. Arms, legs and broomsticks were all in a jumble.

"These brooms are history!"

said Hector, untangling, then brushing himself off.

But he spoke too soon. Right before their eyes the army of broken brooms stood up and each grew back to its original size. The brooms headed for the first floor.

The kids followed.

"We need help," said Hector.

"We've got to find Mr. Bundy," said Nancy.

The brooms were out of control! They were sweeping and re-sweeping the floors.

They were climbing the walls and dancing across the ceiling.

Meanwhile, Mr. Bundy was in the kindergarten class listening to **Alice** read the poem she had written.

"I like flowers.
They have cheering powers.
I like birds.
They sing without words.
I like . . .
BROOMS?
In the halls?"

Alice stopped and stared. Mr. Bundy thought she had finished her poem, and he began to clap.

"Wonderful poem!" he said. "That ending was a refreshing surprise."

"No, there really *are* brooms!" said Alice. "**Look!** They're flying around the hall."

Alice always told the truth, so if she said there were brooms flying in the hall, it had to be true. Everyone turned to look.

"**Eeeek!**" the kids shouted.

Ms. Tilly gathered all of them

behind her to keep them safe.

But she couldn't stop them from

being curious. They kept peeking
out from either side of her, making frightened little noises.

When Mr. Bundy opened the
door to find out what was going
on, a group of brooms zoomed
into the kindergarten. They began

sweeping every **nook** and **cranny**.

More and more teachers opened their doors to see what the **commotion** was about. The brooms swept into their class-rooms. Kids were jumping on chairs and diving under desks. Teachers scolded the brooms as they tried shooing them out. **There was chaos at PS 88!**

Mr. Bundy noticed Roger in the hall

slinking away, looking very guilty. Mr. Bundy stopped him.

"Do you know anything about this?" he asked.

Roger wished he didn't have to tell Mr. Bundy every last detail of the story. But he knew it was the only way to get the school out of the mess he'd made. So he told Mr. Bundy everything as fast as he could.

Mr. Bundy raced to his office. Fighting off the brooms flying around his desk, he found Olivia

Martin's letter with her phone number and quickly called her. **Ring-ring! Ring-ring!** She finally answered on the fourth ring. Thank goodness!

"Olivia Martin, Doctor of Sorcery, here," she said. "Are you ready to put magic in your life?"

"This is Mr. Bundy, principal of PS 88, and we've got way too much magic already. There's an out-of-control army of brooms racing around our school," he said, batting an especially **frisky** broom off his head. "We need help in a hurry!"

5

Breaking the Spell

Mr. Bundy listened carefully to Dr. Martin and took notes on how to break the spell. **"Got it!"** he said. "Thank you."

He ran back out into the hall and did exactly what Olivia

Martin told him to do. He clapped his hands three times and said,

"Zippity, zap!
Zippity, zum!
Thank you, brooms.
Your work is done!"

The brooms froze in their tracks, then disappeared in a cloud of smoke. The only broom left was the one from Mr. Bundy's closet. It fell to the floor just the way a broom should

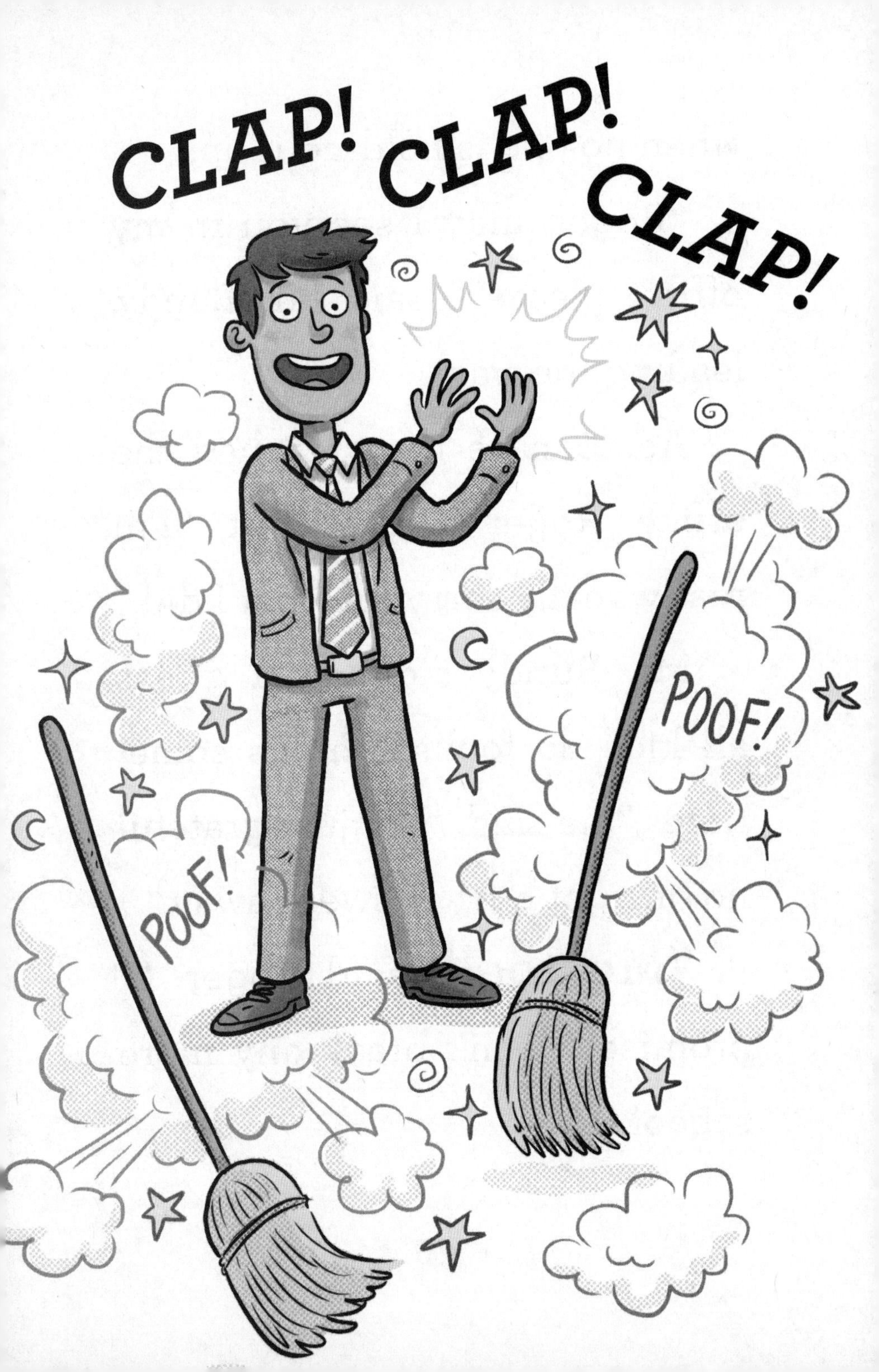
CLAP!
CLAP!
CLAP!
POOF!
POOF!

when no one is holding it up.

"Roger, may I see you in my office, please?" said Mr. Bundy, leading the way.

As soon as they reached the office, Roger **blurted** out, "I'm really, really sorry for what I did."

Mr. Bundy sighed. "I guess all kids do foolish things sometimes," he said. "I'm just grateful no one got hurt or swept away."

"Me too!" said Roger. "I promise I won't break any more school rules."

"I'm going to help you remember that," said Mr. Bundy. "For the next month, you have after-school sweeping duty. I don't mean just your own classroom. I mean the whole school."

"Along with every classroom," he added, "you'll be sweeping the library, the gym, the lunchroom." Mr. Bundy paused. **"And don't forget the bathrooms!"**

When Roger heard "bathrooms," he wanted to run. He wanted to hide! But he stayed right where he was because he knew he deserved it.

Later that week, Mr. Bundy held a special assembly to speak about the importance of following school rules.

"Rules help us get along with one another. They help keep order. They help keep us safe," said Mr. Bundy.

A smile spread across his face as he walked across the stage and **dimmed** the lights.

"Yes, rules are important," he continued. "But sometimes,

rules are meant to be broken."

Olivia Martin, Doctor of Sorcery, came flying across the stage on a glow-in-the-dark broom. As she glided out into the auditorium, she nodded to Mr. Bundy, and together they called,

"Zippity, zap!
Zippity, zoom!
Everybody,
grab a broom!"

They sprinkled magic powder in the air, and suddenly brooms

were floating all around. Every kid and teacher grabbed one and went flying out of the auditorium.

Mr. Bundy led the way. He had done it again. He had made the most exciting assembly program in town.

Word List

blurted (BLUR·ted): Said something suddenly, often without thinking

careening (ca·REEN·ing): Moving quickly from side to side in an uncontrolled way

commotion (cuh·MO·shun): Noise and confusion; a noisy disturbance

cranny (CRAN·nee): A small, narrow space

curiosity (cure·ee·OS·i·tee):
Interest in finding out about
something

dimmed (DIMMED): Made less
bright

frisky (FRI·skee): Playful, lively,
or full of energy

glaring (GLARE·ing): Staring in
an angry way

impressed (im·PRESSED):
Thinking something is great

nook (NOOK): A small, private
corner

resist (ree·ZIST): To stop yourself from doing something you want to do

sanitation (san·i·TAY·shun): The process of keeping places clean and healthy

sorcerer (SOR·ser·er): A magician or wizard

Questions

1. What chore do you dislike the most?

2. Would you like to be the principal's helper? What would you do?

3. If you were a sorcerer, what magic spell would you cast?

4. Imagine you've been given a magic broom. Where will you fly?

5. If you were allowed to break one rule, which rule would it be?

LOOKING FOR A FAST, FUN READ?
BE SURE TO MAKE IT ALADDIN QUIX!

CHUCKLE YOUR WAY THROUGH THESE EASY-TO-READ ILLUSTRATED CHAPTER BOOKS!

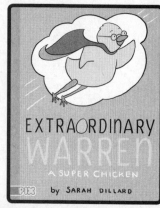

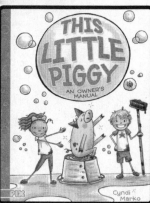

EBOOK EDITIONS ALSO AVAILABLE

FROM ALADDIN
SIMONANDSCHUSTER.COM/KIDS

CHUCKLE YOUR WAY THROUGH THESE EASY-TO-READ ILLUSTRATED CHAPTER BOOKS!

EXTRAORDINARY WARREN
A SUPER CHICKEN
by SARAH DILLARD

EXTRAORDINARY WARREN
SAVES THE DAY
by SARAH DILLARD

SNAIL HAS LUNCH
MARY PETERSON

BUCK'S TOOTH
Diane Kredensor

THIS LITTLE PIGGY
AN OWNER'S MANUAL
Cyndi Marko

EBOOK EDITIONS ALSO AVAILABLE

FROM ALADDIN
SIMONANDSCHUSTER.COM/KIDS